Careers without College

Home Health Aide

by Charnan Simon

Content Consultant:
Debra Arrindall
Director
Home Care Aide Association

C A P S T O N E
H I G H / L O W   B O O K S
an imprint of Capstone Press

C A P S T O N E   P R E S S

818 North Willow Street • Mankato, Minnesota 56001
www.capstone-press.com

Library of Congress Cataloging-in-Publication Data
Simon, Charnan.
    Home health aide/by Charnan Simon.
       p. cm.--(Careers without college)
    Includes bibliographical references and index.
    Summary: Outlines the educational requirements, duties, salary,
employment outlook, and possible future positions of home health aides.
    ISBN 1-56065-704-9
    1. Home health aides--Vocational guidance--Juvenile literature. [1.
Home health aides. 2. Vocational guidance.] I. Title. II. Series: Careers
without college (Mankato, Minn.)
RA645.35.S54 1998
610.69'53--DC21

                                             97-35233
                                             CIP
                                                AC

Photo credits:
CARING/Marilu P. Sherer, 4, 9, 14, 17, 19, 25, 27, 32, 35, 41
International Stock/Ron Maratea, 22; Stan Pak, cover, 11
James L. Shaffer, 36
Unicorn Stock Photos/John L. Ebeling, 12; Rod Furgason, 28; Jeff Greenberg,
   38; A. Ramey, 30; A. Rodham, 20
Valan Photos/John Eastcott and Yva Momatink, 43

Table of Contents

Fast Facts 5

Chapter 1   Job Responsibilities. 7

Chapter 2   What the Job Is Like 15

Chapter 3   Training. 23

Chapter 4   Salary and Job Outlook. 31

Chapter 5   Where the Job Can Lead 37

Words to Know 44

To Learn More 45

Useful Addresses 46

Internet Sites 47

Index 48

Fast Facts

Career Title	Home Health Aide
Minimum Educational Requirement	High school diploma
Certification Requirement	License required in some states
U.S. Salary Range	$10,000 to $34,000
Canadian Salary Range	$7,300 to $46,700 (Canadian dollars)
U.S. Job Outlook	Much faster than the average
Canadian Job Outlook	Faster than the average
DOT Cluster (Dictionary of Occupational Titles)	Service Occupations
DOT Number	354.377-014
GOE Number (Guide for Occupational Exploration)	10.03.03
NOC (National Occupational Classification—Canada)	3413

Chapter 1

Job Responsibilities

Home health aides take care of people who cannot care for themselves. Some of these people are ill. Others have disabled bodies or minds. Home health aides also help people who have just come home from hospitals.

Home health aides help their clients in many ways. A client is a customer. Home health aides cook, clean, and do other household chores. They help their clients bathe and dress. They give

Home health aides help their clients in many ways.

clients medicines. They might help clients walk or drive them to doctors' offices. Home health aides must be calm and friendly. They also must be strong and healthy. Their work can be hard and the pay can be low. Home health aides like their jobs because they know they are helping people.

Clients

People who cannot care for themselves may have to stay in hospitals or nursing homes. But many people would rather stay at home. They prefer familiar settings and privacy. They find comfort and happiness in their own homes. Home health aides make it possible for their clients to stay at home.

Home health aides take care of people in many situations. Some aides work with older people. Many older people think clearly but are not strong. They may need help doing housework. They may need help getting dressed or going shopping.

Home health aides take care of people who cannot take care of themselves.

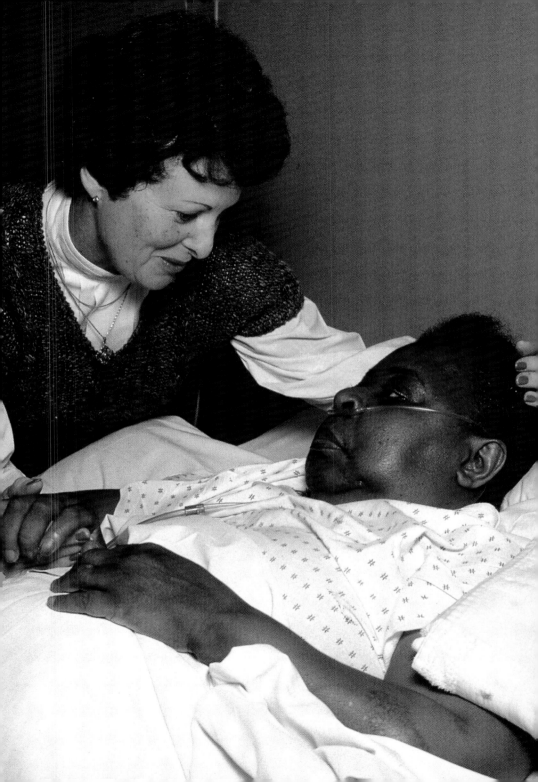

Some older people become confused. They may be forgetful. Home health aides make sure these clients do not harm themselves. They make sure clients eat regularly. They help clients take medicines and keep doctor appointments.

Some aides work with clients who are recovering from surgery. Surgery is repairing or removing parts of the body that are sick or hurt. These clients may be weak. They also may need to stay in bed. Some of these clients may need medicine. They also may need exercise. Some people have suffered brain damage. They need to relearn basic skills. Some need to learn to walk again. Others need to learn to feed themselves.

Aides also help people with developmental disabilities. People with developmental disabilities may be healthy and strong. Often they cannot do household tasks such as cooking or shopping. Home health aides help these people live on their own.

Home health aides help people live on their own.

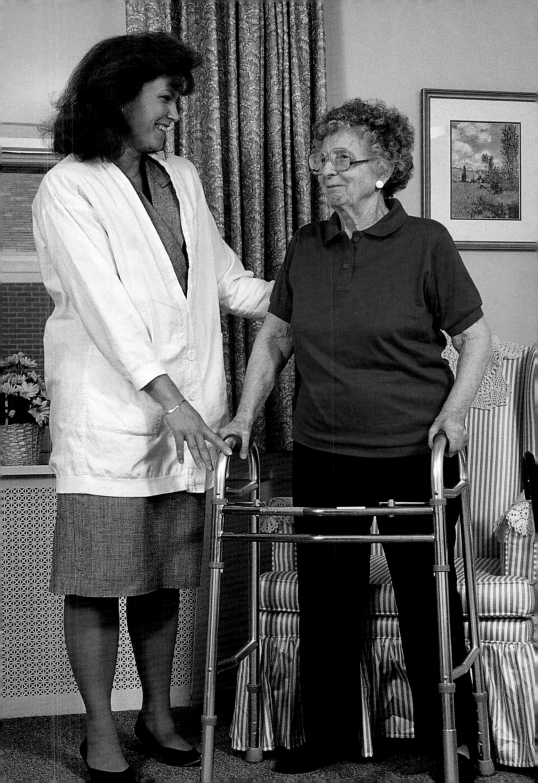

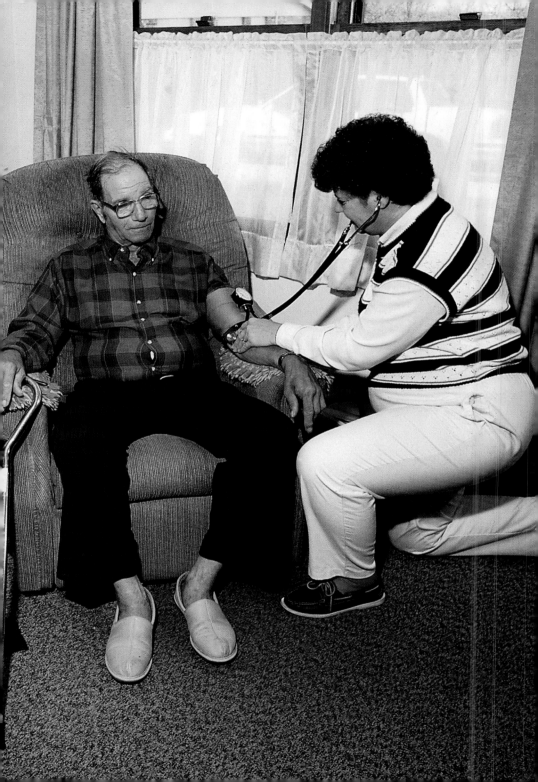

Duties

Home health aides do whatever their clients cannot do for themselves. Aides shop, cook, and clean up after meals. They bathe and dress their clients. Some do laundry and change sheets. Aides may rub clients' sore muscles or give other treatments.

Experienced home health aides may check clients' heart rates. They may take clients' temperatures. They must know how to change bandages. Sometimes home health aides help clients put on leg braces. A brace fastens around a limb to support it. Braces are usually made of metal or plastic. Aides also help clients care for artificial limbs. Artificial means made by people.

Home health aides often talk with their clients. People who are home all the time may be lonely. Aides listen to clients and help them keep a good outlook.

Experienced home health aides may check clients' heart rates.

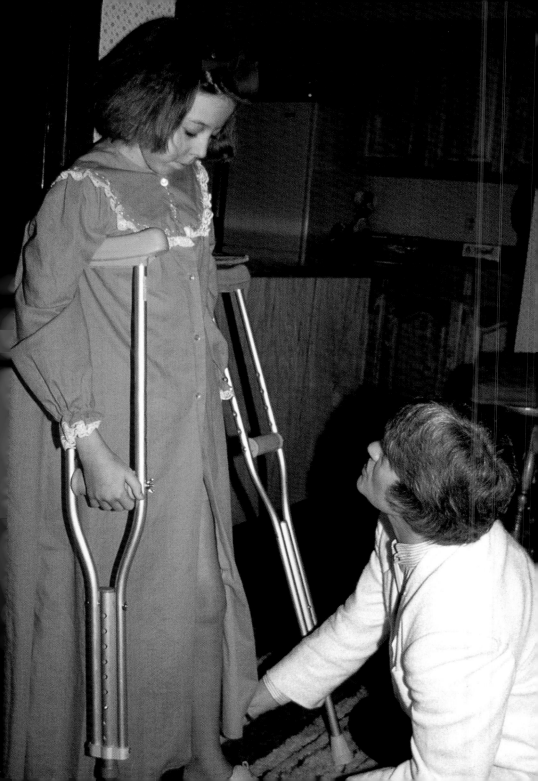

Chapter 2

What the Job Is Like

Some home health aides visit the same client every day. Others see many clients each day. One job may last only a few days. Another job may last weeks or even months. The length of a job depends on clients' needs.

Some clients have problems that do not get better. These people need help all the time. Other clients become well. These clients need care for only a limited time.

Some clients need care for only a limited time.

Hours

Home health aides' work hours vary. Clients often need help early in the morning. These people may need help to get out of bed. They may also need help to wash and dress. These same people may need help again at night.

Home health aides often work on weekends and holidays. Ill people need help every day. Many home health aides work part-time. This allows them to care for their own families or work other jobs.

Much of home health aides' time is spent going from place to place. They must drive or take public transportation from one client's house to another. Aides rarely receive pay for this time.

Work Settings

Every client's needs are different. Every job has different working conditions. Some people live in large homes. Others live in small apartments. Not

Home health aides may wash clients or help them dress.

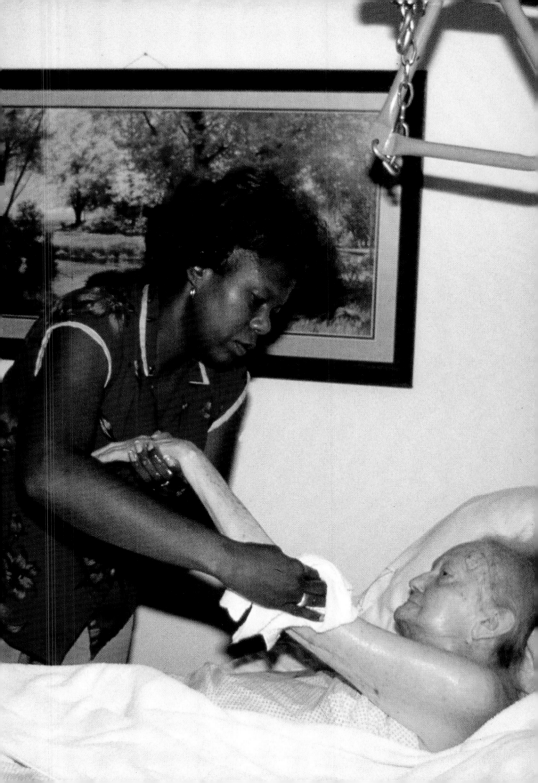

all clients are tidy. Not all people live in clean homes.

Each client is different. Some people are friendly and happy even though they are sick. Other clients may be sad or angry. Home health aides must try to understand their clients. They must learn to work in many different situations.

Important Skills

Home health aides should be neat and clean. They should be strong and healthy. They may have to lift clients out of bathtubs or beds. They may have to push wheelchairs or help people who use walkers. They may have to do tiring housework. Home health aides need plenty of energy to do their jobs well.

Home health aides also keep careful records. They write down all the things they do for their clients. They record changes in their clients' behavior. They keep track of how their clients are feeling.

Home health aides are kind and caring.

Aides show these records to their supervisors. Supervisors are responsible for the work of others. A supervisor might be a nurse or a social worker. The supervisor and the home health aide decide together how to help a client. Home health aides must carry out their supervisors' orders.

Home health aides also must realize the limits of their responsibilities. Home health aides are not doctors or nurses. They cannot decide what the best treatment is for their clients. They must do what doctors and nurses think is best for their patients.

Home health aides often push wheelchairs.

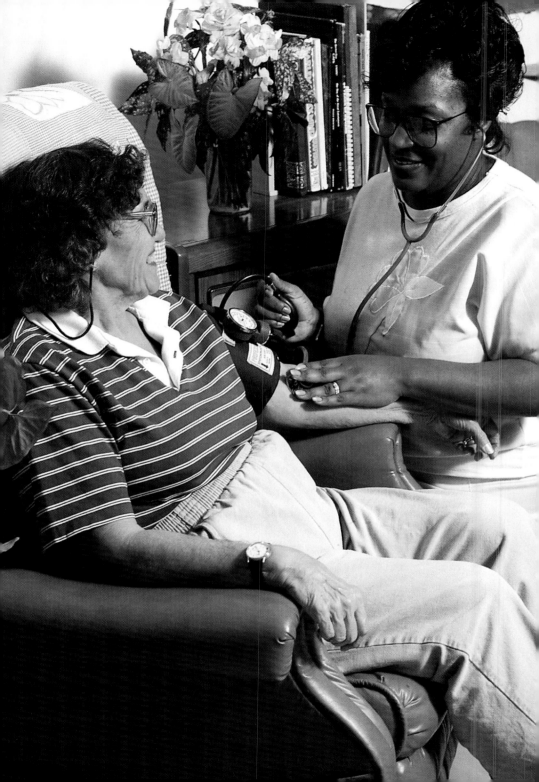

Chapter 3

Training

Required training for home health aides varies from state to state. Some states require certification. Certification is official recognition of a person's abilities and skills. In other states, anyone can work as a home health aide. Students interested in this job should check their states' requirements. Local health-care agencies can help.

Required training for home health aides varies from state to state.

Education

Home health aides must graduate from high school. Home economics, family living, and health classes are useful high school courses.

Most health-care agencies offer classroom training. Students learn about healthy eating and cleanliness. They learn how to work with sad and troubled clients. They study first aid and the basics of health care. They may take courses in how children develop.

Students also practice on-the-job skills. Experienced trainers always supervise students. Sometimes students practice in classrooms. They may work in clients' homes after they gain experience. Students learn how to bathe, dress, and feed patients. They practice lifting and moving clients. They learn how to use wheelchairs, braces, and artificial limbs.

Students practice on-the-job skills.

Home health aides can become certified. They do this by taking extra courses and passing a special exam. The National Association for Home Care awards a certification. Aides with national certification often earn more money.

Personality Traits

Good home health aides share certain traits. They are calm and good-natured. They are kind and caring. They are able to work with both cranky clients and pleasant clients. Aides must overlook rudeness from clients who are in pain. They must understand when their clients are confused. Home health aides often find themselves in sad situations. They need to stay cheerful and helpful.

Home health aides also must be inventive. Working in a home is not the same as working

Home health aides need to stay cheerful and helpful.

in a hospital. Aides may not always have the best tools on hand. They must be able to do their jobs with ordinary household supplies.

Home health aides must be honest. Their clients must be able to trust them. Some clients may not be used to having strangers in their homes. Home health aides learn when their clients need to be alone.

Home health aides must be able to do housework.

Chapter 4

Salary and Job Outlook

Earnings for home health aides vary greatly. Most earn the minimum wage when they begin working. Minimum wage is the lowest amount an employer can pay a worker. Experienced aides can earn up to $10 per hour. Supervisors can earn as much as $18 per hour. Most full-time home health aides earn between $10,000 and $34,000 per year. Beginning aides earn as little as $7,300 per year in Canada.

Most full-time home health aides earn between $10,000 and $34,000 per year.

Home health aides work in many different situations. Many aides work for businesses that provide workers to clients. Some work for nurse groups. Others work for the government.

Some home health aides work for themselves. They find their own clients. They set their own hours and fees.

Benefits

Some large agencies offer benefits to their workers. A benefit is a payment or service in addition to a salary or wages. Full-time home health aides may earn one week of paid vacation after a year of work. They may receive more vacation time after they have more experience.

Most agencies pay home health aides hourly wages. Many agencies do not give aides health insurance, paid vacations, or paid sick leave. Health insurance is protection against the cost of getting sick. People pay a small amount to insurance companies each month. The insurance

Some home health aides find their own clients.

companies will pay most of the bills if a person becomes sick.

Some full-time aides also may receive retirement benefits. Retirement benefits are payments made to people who are no longer working.

Job Outlook

The job outlook for home health aides is very good. The number of people needing home health care is growing. People are living longer. Some of these older people need help in their daily lives. Home health aides give older people the help they need.

Many people also prefer to stay at home if they are ill. Hospitals and nursing homes may try to save people money by moving them home. Treatment in patients' homes is better for them because they are in familiar places. Home health aides help these people get well at home.

Home health aides help people get well at home.

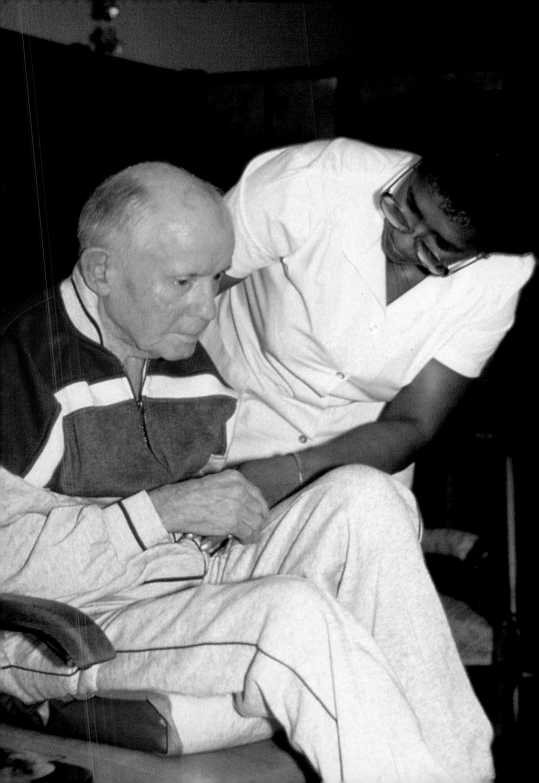

Chapter 5

Where the Job Can Lead

The need for home health aides should continue to grow. People in the United States and Canada are living longer. Many people will need home health care as they age.

Getting Started
Local health care agencies can provide information about becoming a home health aide. Volunteering as an aide at a nursing home

Volunteering as an aide at a nursing home or hospital is a good idea.

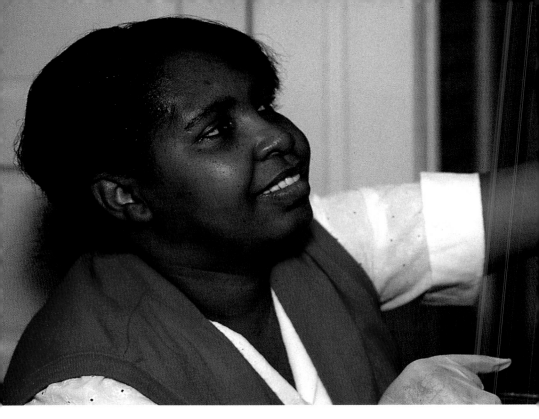

Volunteers can learn what it is like to help ill and disabled people.

or hospital also is a good idea. Volunteer means to offer to do a job without pay. Volunteers can learn what it is like to help ill and disabled people.

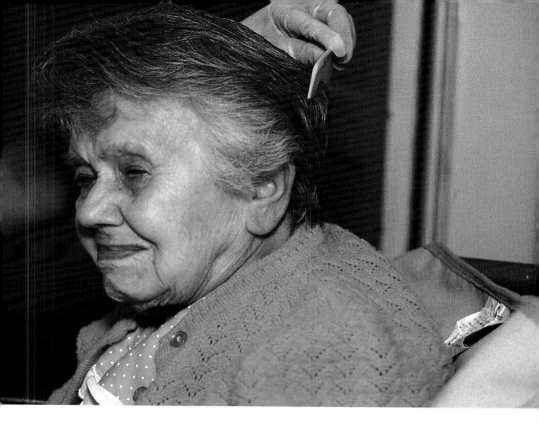

The yellow pages in a telephone book also provide helpful information. People interested in becoming home health aides can look under Home Health Care for a list of agencies. Local chapters of the Red Cross may hire beginning home health aides.

Some agencies hire beginning aides to do basic housecleaning chores. Agencies may allow these aides to handle personal care duties as they gain experience. Aides may receive additional training to learn more about home health care.

Moving Up

Most home health care workers receive regular pay increases as they gain experience. Workers with more training and experience earn more money.

There are not many ways to advance as a home health aide. Some hard-working and experienced aides become supervisors. Others may specialize in working with certain types of clients. For example, aides may become skilled at handling medical equipment such as ventilators. Ventilators force air into and out of patients'

Home health aides may become skilled at handling medical equipment such as ventilators.

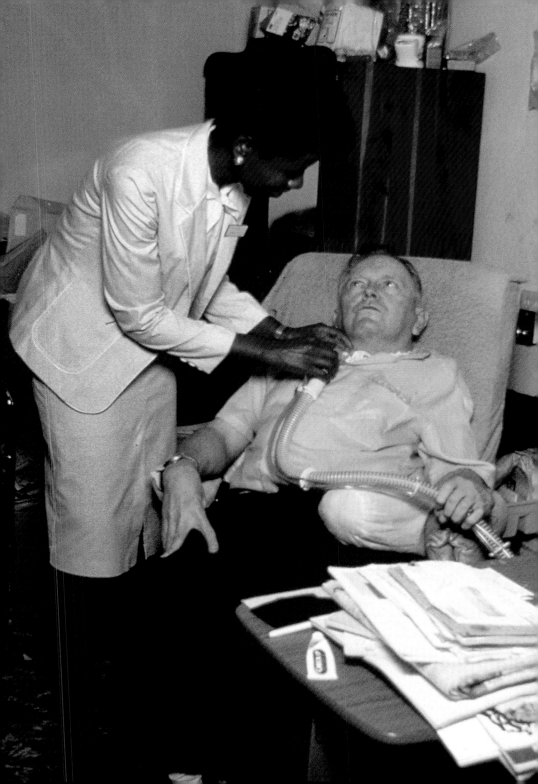

lungs. Skilled specialists and supervisors receive higher wages than other home health aides.

Some home health aides decide to work in related jobs. They may become nurses. They might train to work in hospitals. Aides interested in nutrition could study to become dieticians. A dietician is a person who helps clients eat healthful foods. These jobs all require education and formal training.

The home health care field is growing. Able home health aides are in high demand. But this work is not for everyone. Home health aides work hard in difficult conditions. The work is often stressful. But it can also be very rewarding. Home health aides improve the quality of their clients' lives.

Home health aides improve the quality of their clients' lives.

Words to Know

certification (sur-tif-uh-KAY-shun)—official recognition of a person's abilities and skills

dietician (dye-uh-TI-shun)—a person who helps clients eat healthful foods

health insurance (HELTH in-SHU-ruhnss)—protection from the cost of getting sick

retirement benefits (ri-TIRE-muhnt BEN-uh-fits)—salaries paid to people who are older and no longer working

supervisor (SOO-puyr-vye-zur)—people responsible for the work of others

volunteer (vol-uhn-TIHR)—to offer to do a job without pay

To Learn More

Lee, Barbara. *Working in Health Care and Wellness.* Minneapolis: Lerner Publications Co., 1996.

Paradis, Adrian A. *Careers for Caring People and Other Sensitive Types.* Lincolnwood, Ill.: VGM Career Horizons, 1996.

Wilkinson, Beth. *Careers Inside the World of Health Care.* New York: Rosen Publishing Group, 1995.

Zucker, Elana D., ed. *Being a Homemaker/Home Health Aide.* Upper Saddle River, N.J.: Prentice Hall, 1998.

Useful Addresses

Home Care Association of America, Inc.
9570 Regency Square Blvd.
Jacksonville, FL 32225

National Association for Home Care
228 7th Street SE
Washington, DC 20003

World Homecare and Hospice Organization
228 7th Street SE
Washington, DC 20003

Internet Sites

HCAA Home Page
http://www.hcaa-homecare.com/

Home Health Aides
http://www.state.sd.us/state/executive/dol/sdooh/
 adltchcr/homheaad.htm

Homemaker—Home Health Aides
http://stats.bls.gov/oco/ocos173.htm

NAHC's Home Page
http://www.nahc.org/

Index

artificial limb, 13, 24

brace, 13, 24

certification, 23, 26

developmental disabilities, 10
dietician, 42
disabled, 7, 38
duties, 13, 40

education, 24-26, 42
exercise, 10

health insurance, 33
hospital, 7, 8, 29, 34, 38, 42
hours, 16, 33
housework, 8, 18

job outlook, 34

National Association for
  Home Care, 26

Red Cross, 40
retirement, 34

supervisor, 21, 24, 31, 40, 42
surgery, 10

temperature, 13

ventilator, 40
volunteer, 37, 38

wheelchair, 18, 24
work settings, 16-18